A

B

Dedicated to the memory of my adventurous sister, Deb.

Southwood Books Limited
3-5 Islington High Street
London N1 9LQ

First published in Australia in 2002 by ABC Books for
The Australian Broadcasting Corporation
GPO Box 9994 Sydney NSW 2001

This edition published in the UK under licence from ABC Books by
Southwood Books Limited, 2002

Copyright © text and illustrations Judith Rossell 2002

ISBN 1 903207 70 3

A CIP catalogue record for this book is available from the British Library.

Set in Bembo
Designed by Kerry Klinner
Colour separations by PageSet, Victoria
Printed and bound by Tien Wah Press, Singapore

5 4 3 2 1

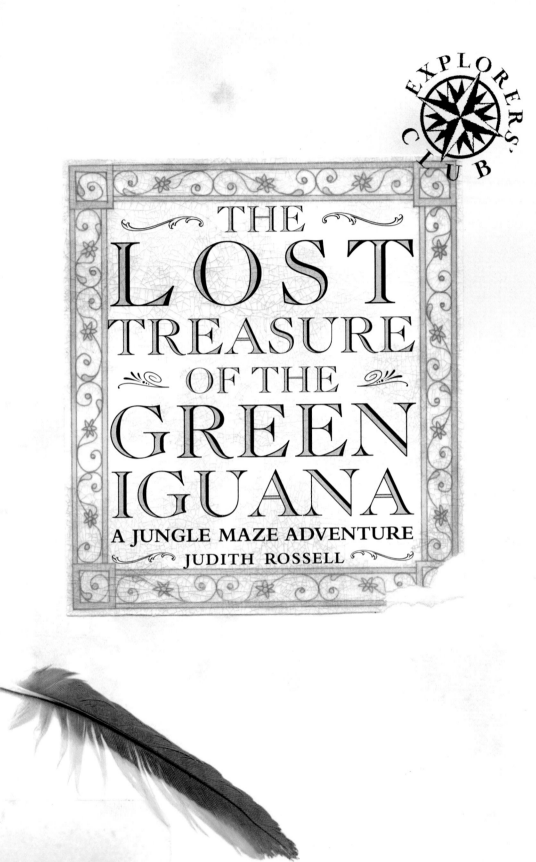

THE LOST TREASURE OF THE GREEN IGUANA

A JUNGLE MAZE ADVENTURE

JUDITH ROSSELL

EXPLORERS CLUB

SOUTHWOOD
BOOKS

PASADERA

The President
Explorers' Club

The President
Explorers' Club
99 Intrepid St
Valeroso

Dear President,

I hope you can send one of your members to help us. Our famous scientist, Dr Fortuito, has disappeared. He set out a month ago on his fourteenth expedition to seek the legendary "Lost Treasure of the Green Iguana". We are very concerned for his safety because he promised to return for our midsummer festival and there is still no sign of him.

Attached is a recent photograph of Dr Fortuito from the "Pasadera Post". I am also sending you a folder containing some of the Doctor's notes about the flora and fauna of this area. The jungle around Pasadera is notoriously dangerous, but these notes will help. We are offering a huge reward for the Doctor's safe return, so please send one of your members with all speed!

Yours sincerely,

Bela Pomposo

Mrs B. Pomposo
Mayor
Pasadera

Fourteenth Time Lucky?

"Fourteen has always been a lucky number for me," said Dr Fortuito, before setting out today on his fourteenth expedition to find the Lost Treasure of the Green Iguana. Just released from hospital after recovering from his thirteenth attempt, Dr Fortuito was

EXPLORERS' CLUB

Dear Explorer,

This urgent request arrived today from the Mayor of Pasadera. A scientist, Dr Fortuito, has vanished while searching for the Lost Treasure of the Green Iguana. With a bit of luck, you should be able to find the treasure as well as the missing scientist.

My advice is to study the Doctor's folder of notes very carefully. The jungle around Pasadera is full of dangers — Giant Water Snails, crocodiles, poisonous snakes, Savage Snake Vines and even hippos! The notes will help you deal with anything that blocks your path.

Be prepared for a long trek, the jungle is a maze of interconnecting paths and there is no map. You will probably need to retrace your steps many times.

Best of luck for a successful expedition.

Lily Leyenda

President
Explorers' Club

Legendary Lost Treasure

The fabulous Lost Treasure of the Green Iguana is one of the greatest mysteries of our time. Originally hidden by pirates, it is believed to be in the vicinity of the ruined city of Las Cabezas. Legends tell of a ferocious Giant Green Iguana that stands guard over the treasure. The only known way to overcome this creature is to startle it away with a swarm of Red Jewel Beetles. At least ten beetles must be collected in order to frighten away the Iguana and lay claim to the treasure.

http://lostloot.com/SouthAmerica/history/legend253.asp

I found this on the Net, I hope it is useful!
Lily

Is it all clear? You need to find the lost scientist and the treasure. Use the notes on both the folder flaps to help you overcome any dangers that block your way and keep your eyes open for items along the path that you will need later. When you reach the edge of a page, turn to the page number there and keep going. Do not leave the path. Good Luck!

Start here ⟶

3
←